GYMNASTICS JAM

Martha Louise

Illustrations by Carol Watson

Frey House Publishing, LLC
Ponte Vedra Beach, FL

Book and cover design by Sagaponack Books & Design

Cover art by Carol Watson

ISBNs:
978-1-7329423-3-2 (softcover)
978-1-7329423-4-9 (hardcover)
978-1-7329423-5-6 (e-book)

Library of Congress Catalog Number: 2021915086

Summary: To advance a level in gymnastics, Adeline must join a team in a new gym. Her greatest challenge should be achieving the skills and scoring high, but when she meets two unwelcoming teammates, they shake her confidence and trigger a tumble of emotions.

JUV045000 Juvenile Fiction / Readers / Chapter Books
JUV032200 Juvenile Fiction / Sports & Recreation / Gymnastics
JUV039050 Juvenile Fiction / Social Themes / Emotions & Feelings
JUV014000 Juvenile Fiction /Girls & Women

www.MarthaLouise.net

Printed and bound in the USA
First Edition

To my three athletic and talented daughters, Jamie, Alyson, and Lindsey, whose real-life experiences helped create Adeline.

Contents

Chapter One

She felt hypnotized. Adeline gazed out the passenger window of her mother's SUV as it raced by a green wooded area. The tween watched the trees flash by, noticing the patterned stripes of speckled brown and green merging and fanning out as they passed. She halfway listened to her mother apologizing for running late *again*. Adeline shook her head. She knew it would not be the last time her mother overlooked the clock.

"I couldn't get away. Teachers are always seeking the school counselor—all day and especially at the end of the day. Before I could shut and lock my door after the last bell rang, they were there."

As late as Mrs. Lawrence sometimes was, Adeline could imagine twenty teachers lined up outside her door.

Wednesday was her mother's carpool day and for her to get four eager gymnasts to their gym practice on time, she had to leave school promptly at 3:30 p.m. She was never on time for the beginning of the twenty-two-mile drive. In fact, she was never on time for anything!

Not her usual cheerful self on this trip, Adeline had mixed emotions about her last practice session in the gym. She felt as if her sad, happy, excited, and doubtful feelings were all thrown into a bowl and stirred, round and round, until it was making her dizzy. Maybe that was why she was in a daze.

She'd soon be at this gym for the last time. She would be joining another gymnastics team whose gym was closer to her home. Although she knew she wanted to make the move, she was feeling unhappy about leaving her friends at this—her very first—gym.

Gymnastics was Adeline's life! She enjoyed the tumbling, the body workouts, the six-pack she was developing, and she liked all the girls on her Jacksonville Gymnastics' level 4 team. At the beginning of the year, she had set a goal to move up to level 5 after the competing season. However, to her dismay, her coach decided to keep the team at level 4.

"Gosh, Adeline,"—Reese's voice from the back seat broke into her thoughts—"don't you want to think about this some more? We will all miss you, and you *know* you will miss us," she said, deliberately raising her eyebrows. "Besides that,"—she crossed her arms and lowered her brows—"you won't be there when we make high scores next season. Our coach says we'll be sure to score 9.0 or higher since it's our second season at the same level."

Carter chimed in, using the same disgruntled tone. "And we also need you for the team's first place trophy."

Tiring of the level 4 routine, Adeline had asked her mother a month earlier if they could visit other gyms. Mrs. Lawrence swiftly complied, keen to cut the distance she had to drive, and they visited several other facilities. Two of the gyms were farther than Jacksonville Gymnastics. Mrs. Lawrence and Adeline decided on the closest one, East Coast Gymnastics. Three of East Coast's coaches had been on a Russian Olympic team, which had impressed both Adeline and her mother.

The East Coast coach who had observed Adeline at her trial session told her mother Adeline was ready for level 5 and possibly a higher level. At least that was what Adeline's mother thought he said. Adeline was standing nearby and heard the same thing; she also had trouble understanding Coach Les because of his strong Russian accent.

Several times while he was speaking, she glanced at her mother with question marks clouding her eyes. *Is he speaking Russian?*

Even though Adeline was excited about the new gym, she was feeling uncertain about leaving her old team and their tight friendship circle.

"Yes," Adeline answered as she twisted her upper body to see her teammates. "You *will* score high. Even so, I want to learn new things. I don't care if I make 7s and 8s at level 5. At least I'll be learning different skills and performing a new routine."

A 10.0 score was a perfect number on the scoreboard, and most gymnasts were happy to receive at least 8.0. The top scores achieved at the meets were 9.0 and higher, with the most competitive performers watching for those digits to flash across the screen. Well, not just the most competitive. All gymnasts wished for those scores.

Adeline untwisted to face the windshield. She would not tell Reese and Carter she secretly hoped to score high 8s in level 5. While she knew she couldn't possibly make a 9 in any other event, she thought she had a chance in the vault. She had used the handspring vault for the first time at a meet in South Carolina and had scored an 8.1. With good instruction—which she felt she would be getting from the former Russian Olympic team members—she was bound to score higher.

The coach at the gym in South Carolina was a friend of her coach at Jacksonville Gymnastics in Florida, and Adeline's team had been invited to compete at the meet. Adeline's mother didn't want her to go because Adeline would have to miss a day of school. Adeline remembered how she had begged and begged, and her mother finally said yes.

Mrs. Lawrence had not felt comfortable saying no to the trip and had stalled, unable to give a yes or no answer. A nagging *something* was gnawing at her, and she couldn't get her hands on it to toss it off. And certainly, she couldn't put her finger on it. She and Adeline found that "something" at the meet. Adeline's level 4 performance carried her to first place in the all-around, after winning medals in all four events for her age group. Achieving a total score of 35.0 made the trip more exciting than she had dreamed possible.

Adeline laughed out loud. Her mother turned her head for a brief second.

"Gee, Mom," Adeline said, and giggled. "I was thinking about the South Carolina trip and how you thought you were psycho."

"Psychic," her mother said while watching the road in front of her. "And that is not the correct term, either. I have a strong sixth sense," she said, using her "Don't make fun of your mother" tone. Why do you think I have the career I have? I'm intuitive. I have to be sensitive to what children may be thinking or feeling, to do the kind of work I do." Realizing she was starting one of her lectures, she stopped herself and asked, "What about the South Carolina trip?"

"I was thinking about the meet," Adeline replied. "How you felt something," she said in a spooky tone, playfully poking her finger into her mother's side, "and you couldn't say no to the trip.

When I placed first, you thought that was what was keeping you from saying no. If we hadn't gone, I wouldn't have made those high scores." Adeline hesitated before adding, "Or any of us." She spun around to Reese and Carter and leaned over the center console, extending her right hand, palm facing the rear seat. Both girls reached out and slapped it, giving her a high five.

Adeline's level 4 team had walked out of the South Carolina gym with the first place trophy. Adeline, Reese, and Carter had all scored high enough to claim the highly desired prize for the team.

Both Reese's and Carter's expressions showed their joy in being reminded of that special day. Then Reese's countenance suddenly changed.

Pressing her lips into a straight line, Reese said in a scolding tone, "We need you, Adeline. Look how much fun that was. I bet your new team won't bring first place trophies home."

"Oh well," Adeline said, "probably not."

Yet, inside she was thinking, *What if we do? Fat chance,* she told herself, and spun back to the front to prepare for the team's goodbyes.

Chapter Two

"It wasn't that bad, Dad," Adeline said. Her father had asked how her last day at Jacksonville Gymnastics had been. Adeline and her mother had just arrived home, and Mr. Lawrence was putting the finishing touches on the family's dinner.

Strolling through the kitchen, Adeline inhaled a whiff of charred beef before she saw the platter of grilled steak strips on the counter. She scowled at it. Steak was not one of her favorites. She was probably the one person in the whole entire world who did not like this meat. Even her three-year-old sister, Charlotte, liked steak. Mr. Lawrence always cut Charlotte's steak into tiny pieces, and Adeline wondered if she'd like it better if her father cut hers the same way.

After setting a full plate in front of Adeline's mother at the dining room table, Mr. Lawrence placed Adeline's dish in front of her. "Let me get the last dishes and then I want to hear all about it," he said, and retraced his steps into the kitchen.

Crinkling her nose at the smoky, brown, crusted piece of meat, Adeline stated, "I think I'll become a veterinarian."

Adeline's father reentered the room with his and Charlotte's plates and exclaimed, "Why, Adeline, I've never heard you say that before! You really want to be a veterinarian?"

Her mother, seated across from Adeline, had been watching her. She peered up at her husband and said, "I think she means a vegetarian."

"Oops! I forgot how much you dislike steak," Mr. Lawrence said as he set Charlotte's plate in front of her and began cutting the meat. "I'm sorry, Adeline. I would have prepared something else if I had remembered. This is a special night for you. You are no longer a Jacksonville Gymnastics gymnast, and you have *vaulting* ambition."

"Dad!" Adeline screwed up her mouth and nose, then smirked at her father's attempt at humor.

Mr. Lawrence finished making bite-sized pellets out of Charlotte's steak and slid into his seat at the table. Adeline's appetite for the meat diminished further at the sight of what now appeared to be dried dog food resting alongside Charlotte's green beans and carrots.

Why haven't I noticed that before? she wondered. *Nope, forget about having MY steak cut up.*

"Okay," Mr. Lawrence said as he unfolded his dinner napkin, giving his full attention to Adeline. "I'm ready to hear how today went."

"As I was saying," Adeline replied, stabbing at her meat with her knife, "it wasn't that bad. We had the usual practice and our coach worked us hard. We didn't have time to think about anything else. When it was all over, I gave everybody hugs and said goodbye. It wasn't as hard as I thought it would be."

"Good," her father said. "I didn't want you to feel too sad about leaving."

"I wasn't there that long—at least not long on my team," Adeline replied. She had begun level 4 competition the past year and had been with her teammates one season. "Besides," she said, "I'm really excited about my new gym."

"Let's not get too enthusiastic, Adeline," Mr. Lawrence said as he winked at his wife. "Your food is getting cold, and you don't need to lose your appetite. You need the strength for your higher-level gymnastics."

"Dad!" Adeline muttered, chuckling as she picked up her fork. "I still want to be a—what's the word, Mom? Vegerian?"

"Vegetarian," Mrs. Lawrence replied.

Two days later Adeline and her mother entered East Coast Gymnastics for Adeline's first team practice. The gymnasium was housed inside a spacious gray building and it had an outer waiting room where some of the parents sat and viewed the practice through a large window.

"Hi," Adeline said to a couple of girls standing inside the door that connected the waiting room to the gym.

The girls glanced at Adeline, neither saying a word. One of them whispered something to the other, and they laughed as they walked away.

With her inner alarm jingling, Mrs. Lawrence watched Adeline, who shrugged and headed to the snack area. Adeline slid out of her backpack and placed it and her sports bottle on a table that was covered with colorful bottles and packs.

Mrs. Lawrence marveled at her daughter. Few things upset her, and Mrs. Lawrence was surprised anew by Adeline's resilience. She had always had the ability to bounce back in situations that would normally disturb other children.

"I'll see you later, Adeline," Mrs. Lawrence called to her. "I'll be waiting for you at the end of practice."

"Okay, Mom, I'll be here," Adeline said with a mischievous dance of her eyebrows, before she twirled around and moved into the gym.

Adeline spotted her coach across the large room. He noticed her and waved for her to come over.

"Girls," Coach Les was saying as Adeline approached, "zees ees ze new girl I vas telling you about. Welcome to our gym, Adeline."

"Hi," Adeline said to the group standing in front of her.

Several girls said hi, and Adeline recognized two she had met the day she was observed. The two she saw when she entered the building were in the group and they stood motionless, giving her a cold-eyed stare.

"Okay," Coach Les said, clapping his hands, "let's vork out."

The girls immediately moved into the conditioning drills, first running in a line the full length of the gym. One of the older girls was the leader and took them through an obstacle course. They hopped onto mats and completed several stretch jumps with arms pointing to the ceiling, jogged through narrow pathways lined by more mats, ran in place with high knees, and finished in a heavy-breathing mass.

Next, they held straddle holds, then pike holds, and finally, splits. After thirty minutes, Coach Les gave them a water break and said to return to individual coaches for specific skills training.

Adeline was out of breath as she headed to the snack area. *That was a great workout,* she thought, realizing how easy her first gym's warm-up had been. She had never gotten out of breath before. This gym was already proving to be superior.

She took a large swallow from her sports bottle, feeling her thirst fading as the fluid trickled down her throat. She noticed the two unfriendly girls enter the room.

At the table they picked up their condensation-frosted bottles and began drinking, taking in large gulps of cold water. Adeline saw how out of breath they were and was surprised. She figured most of the girls at this gym had been doing the workout for a long enough time and were used to it. She wanted to ask how long they had been there, but she felt nervous and was afraid they would snub her again.

Both girls drank their water without saying a word. Adeline wondered if they would ever take a breath. They were gulping the water so fast! She sipped hers slowly, as she had been taught, while keeping them in her sight. Other girls came and went, although the two did not seem to notice. Finally, they each stopped and gasped loudly, taking in big mouthfuls of air.

"He works us too hard," one of the girls managed to utter between inhales.

"For sure," the second one said, and bent over, placing her hands on her knees, gasping and exhaling large breaths as she spoke. "He's … trying … to kill us."

Adeline set her bottle down slowly and shook off the jittery feeling creeping into her body.

When she returned to the large gymnasium, she asked, while trying to appear cheerful, "Where do I go, Coach?"

"Over zere veeth Coach Mia, to vork on bar routine." Coach Les pointed to the other coach, who was standing near the uneven bars.

Adeline skipped over to the bars and was followed by the two heavy-breathing, out-of-shape unfriendlies and two other girls she had not yet met.

When they were all gathered in front of her, Coach Mia welcomed Adeline and asked if she knew the other girls' names.

"No, ma'am," she replied, and heard a snicker behind her.

"Thees ees your level 5 team." Coach Mia nodded to the group behind her. "Meet your teammates."

Adeline felt relief. *At least her accent is not as strong as the head coach's!*

"Macey and Harper," Coach Mia said, gesturing to the two short-winded girls.

Coach Mia then pointed to the others and said, "And Olivia and Keely."

Adeline groaned inwardly while turning and raising her head to the four girls, and then flashed her brightest smile.

Like it or not, she thought, *these are my new teammates.*

Chapter Three

Mrs. Lawrence entered the outer room to the gym where Adeline was gathering up her hand grips, pack, and bottle. "Hi, Adeline. How did it go?"

"Fine." Adeline kept her head down, fidgeting with her grips, before placing them in her backpack. She looked up. "Are we going straight home?"

"When do we ever do that?" her mother asked. "No, dear, I have to make a stop at the Town Center on the way."

"Mom," Adeline cried, "you had three hours to shop! What could you possibly need?"

"I forgot to return something of your dad's," Mrs. Lawrence replied innocently. "It will merely take a minute."

As they were driving to the open-air mall, Adeline told her mother about her new teammates. "Can you believe those two—the ones when we first got there—are actually on my team?" Her tone was gloomy. "Not at all friendly."

"Right," her mother said. "Quite unfriendly. I felt bad for you. However, you didn't seem all that bothered by them."

"I wasn't, at first. Then when I found out they were on my team …." Her words trailed off and she lowered her voice. "Besides, they make me feel kind of nervous."

Mrs. Lawrence pulled into Dillard's parking lot and eased into a space. She stopped the engine.

"Adeline," her mother said quietly, rotating her body toward her. "Sometimes you have to be the one to make the first move when seeking a friendship—"

"Mom," Adeline said, "I don't want to be their friend if that's the way they act to other kids."

"You don't have to be their *best* friend," her mother said. "You do have to get along with them on the team, though, right?"

Adeline answered slowly, "Yeah, I guess so."

"I think," her mother said, "you may have to be a little friendlier with them. Show them what a neat kid you are, and they can't help but like you." She tilted her head slightly, her tenderness showing. "And if not, you can at least feel good about how you have acted with them. If they continue being rude to you, they are the ones with the problems, and you probably won't be able to do anything to change them. If you—"

"Okay, okay, Mom," Adeline said, using a friendly tone to stop her. "I got it!" Even though she was accustomed to these types of conversations with her mother, Adeline was always amused when her mother turned counselor on her.

"Come on," her mother said. She reached under her seat and withdrew a medium-sized package. "Let's get this done so we can go home."

They entered Dillard's, and Adeline's mother led her to the men's department.

"What are you returning?" Adeline asked, trailing behind her.

"A package of boxer shorts for a different size," her mother replied as she beelined to the men's underwear section.

Mrs. Lawrence picked up several packages, turning each one over and returning it to its place.

Adeline became restless and said, “Mom, come on! Just get one. Here.” She grabbed a package with brightly colored circles shining beneath the clear plastic and shoved it into her mother’s hand. “Here, Mom, get this one.”

Her mother poked the sparkling spheres and frowned. “Hmm. I don’t think he’d be dazzled,” she said slowly, and grinned at her daughter. “However,” she said, choosing a package with a small red-and-black plaid design, “I’ll get these for him.”

“Wonderful!” Adeline said, reaching behind her head, tossing it and her braid at the same time.

After her mother made the exchange, Adeline strolled with her to the exit. When they reached the door, she stopped, raised her face to her mother, and asked, “Why doesn’t Daddy do his own shopping?”

Before her mother could answer, Adeline announced loudly, “I hope when I’m a wife, I don’t have to buy *my* husband’s underwear.”

An elderly couple shuffled through the doorway at that moment, chuckling as they passed. Adeline ducked her head and hurriedly stepped outside.

On the way home Mrs. Lawrence once more brought up the subject of the gym and made suggestions to her daughter about how she could make the first move.

"I think, Adeline, when you are all taking a break and they're talking about something, try to jump in. Make a comment about whatever they're talking about, and surely they will respond to you. They can't ignore you when you are simply trying to get into a conversation with them."

"Okay, Mom," Adeline said, and sighed audibly. "I'll try and see what happens."

Soon after they arrived home, Adeline took a shower and washed her hair. She breathed in the exotic aroma of coconut mixed with pineapple as she shampooed, allowing the fragrance to relax her. Despite the conditioner she used, she had lots of tangles in her hair when she was finished. Wrapped in a towel, she stood in front of the bathroom mirror and yanked at the knots. *There goes my relaxation.* With her thoughts turning to her gymnastics team, she yanked harder. She jerked on a particularly stubborn lump of twisted hair and yelled, "Ouch!"

Adeline set her comb down and stared into the mirror. *How am I supposed to make the first move,* she thought, *when those two are as rude as they are?*

She studied her reflection. *You appear harmless enough,* she told herself. Her straight red hair fell a few inches below her shoulders. Her hair had been lightened by the Florida sun, and her mother always told her it reminded her of spun gold.

Focusing on her features, she lightly tapped her small nose with her index finger. It was pushed up slightly like a pug's, with a splattering of freckles across it. She lowered her finger to her lips. Her mouth was average, but her smile brightened her entire face.

Her ocean blue, almond-shaped eyes were usually sparkling.

Not tonight.

She lowered her hand and curved her lips down into a frown. She curled them up into a smile. She showed surprise and lifted her brows. She drew them back down, squinted, and changed her expression to one that appeared mean and ugly.

Ooh, scary. She tried it a second time and wrinkled her nose, opening her mouth wide into an ugly growl.

Good, she thought, *if those two ever do anything truly mean to me, this will surely scare them away.*

Turning from the mirror, Adeline threw on a T-shirt and shorts. She bounced down the stairs and found her mother preparing a snack supper for her. Adeline and her mother didn't get home until after 7:30 p.m. on gym nights, and when her father was unable to cook, her mother often prepared a special meal for her.

Carrot sticks and apple slices were piled on a plate on the kitchen counter. White creamy dressing lay in a small dish near the plate. Her mother's back was to her, bent over behind the counter, pulling a tray of pizza bagels out of the oven. A warm breeze, carrying hints of baked dough and garlicky tomato sauce, drifted from her direction.

"Hey," her mother said when she straightened, noticing her daughter, "I wondered what was keeping you."

"I was practicing looking mean," Adeline said. She picked up a carrot stick. Making the ugly growl, she said, "If those two mean girls mess with me, I'll have to use this on 'em. *This*"—she pointed to her face—"not the carrot."

"Adeline," her mother said, watching her while placing the bagels on a plate. She leaned across the counter and set the dish in front of her daughter. She stayed in that position, nose-to-nose with Adeline, and said, "That is not what we were talking about earlier. You can't become what they are. You are you, and you are not mean."

"Well, thank you!" Adeline grinned slyly at her mother. "Don't worry, Mom. I'm only kidding. I don't think I've ever scared anyone. Besides, I don't think those two would scare easily."

Chapter Four

During her next practice session at the gym, Adeline worked harder than ever. She had always wanted to be a good gymnast and found the new coaching staff extremely helpful. She took their instruction to heart, and she achieved skills she had not yet been able to perform. She decided if she worked to be an excellent gymnast, her new teammates would be happy to have her on the team.

While she was practicing her beam routine, Adeline noticed Macey and Harper watching her. She tried to shake off the fluttery feeling in her stomach. *Why do they make me so nervous?*

Attempting to get them out of her mind, she concentrated on each move, and when she managed to get through the half backward swing turn without faltering, she felt instant relief. It had failed her many times during practice. She often lost her balance and leaned to the side, as if she needed to greet her lower half. *Hello, legs!*

Coach Mia applauded, and Adeline blushed.

"Thet was the best I hev seen you do thus far!" Coach Mia said as she walked over to the beam. To the other level 5 girls, she said, "I hope you all saw thet." She gestured as she spoke. "Eef you girls vould vork es hard es Adeline, we could hev a *great* team!"

Adeline was dismayed. *What happened to Coach Mia's accent?*

And why is she doing this to me?

Macey and Harper had their eyes fixed on their coach before their line of vision switched to Adeline. They glared at her.

Great! Adeline thought. *This is not at all what I need. I want them to like me, not hate me!*

"Come on, girls," Coach Mia said in a commanding tone. "Everyone else gets one more turn et the beam. Adeline, you can hev your vater break."

Feeling embarrassed that Coach had held her up as a model example, Adeline casually moved away from the group, toward the snack area. At the gym exit, she glanced over her shoulder in time to see Harper lose her balance on the beam and hop to the floor.

A few minutes later Harper and Macey entered the room. Harper asked Macey what she thought about the movie they had recently watched together. Adeline recognized the movie and decided she'd try what her mother had suggested.

She took a step toward them and said, "That was such a good movie! It's one of my favorites. What did you think about the—"

"Get lost, Carrot Top!" Harper said sharply. She stared directly at Adeline.

Adeline could not hold back her surprise. *Carrot Top! Why is she calling me that? Carrot tops are green!*

Her second thought quickly followed: *No one has ever talked to me like this.* Most girls she knew acted nice enough, and she had never encountered outright rudeness. Dumbfounded, she couldn't think of anything to say.

After several seconds, Harper turned away from Adeline, shrugged, and resumed her conversation with Macey. Neither girl gave any more attention to Adeline.

Finishing her drink, Adeline thought, *How am I ever going to deal with these two?* She was not used to this type of behavior and was stumped.

She wondered, *What else can I do?*

That night after her father took her home, Adeline rushed into the kitchen. Her mother was preparing dinner. The scent of barbeque chicken wings greeted her nose, but she couldn't inhale and revel in it like she normally did.

As soon as she found her mother, Adeline burst into tears and cried, "Now look what you've done!"

Before her mother could say a word, Adeline blurted out, "Mom, it was awful! I did exactly what you said. Harper and Macey were talking about a movie they saw together, and I told them it was one of my favorites. I started to ask them about a part in it, and—" Adeline stopped talking for a second and wiped at her streaming tears.

"Honey," her mother said, "I am proud of you—"

"No, Mom, wait," Adeline cried. "No, it was horrible! When I said that to them, Harper looked straight at me and said, 'Get lost.' " Adeline omitted the Carrot Top part. *What was the use?*

"She actually told me to get lost," Adeline said, her voice rising in anguish. "I could not believe it. No one has ever treated me like that."

Upon hearing her daughter's words, Mrs. Lawrence said, "I can hardly believe it myself. What did you do?"

"What else could I do?" Adeline wailed. "I stood there and finished my drink. They ignored me, and I kept gulping my water. As upset as I was, I didn't let *them* know."

"Thanks, Mom," she added in a sarcastic tone. "I probably wouldn't have said anything to them if you hadn't told me to try something like that."

Mrs. Lawrence raised her hands and rubbed the back of her neck before she placed steady hands on Adeline's shoulders. Steering her to a stool at the kitchen counter, Mrs. Lawrence took the seat next to her.

"Adeline, I can tell how distressed you are," she said. "I'm sorry it didn't work out the way it should have. I think you did the right thing, though. Anyone else would have let you join in and would have talked to you."

Mrs. Lawrence shook her head and added, "I certainly don't understand those two."

"But that's not all of it," Adeline said as her mother pulled her into a hug. She rested her head on her mother's shoulder. "Coach Mia pointed me out as a good example of hard work a few minutes before that happened." Adeline changed her voice and mimicked, " 'Eef you girls vould vork es hard es Adeline.' Maybe they were still mad about that. Anyways, why would my coach do that to me? No one wants to hear anything like that about a teammate. Unless she wanted to hurt me.

"That's it!" Adeline exclaimed, jerking her head back and pushing away from her mother. "She wants them to hate me. Why else would she say that to them?"

"Stop, Adeline. You are letting your imagination get the best of you," Mrs. Lawrence said. "All this is making you a bit anxious, and I can tell you Coach Mia would not do that. I suspect she was trying to give them incentive to work harder, and she, unfortunately, chose the wrong words. She certainly didn't mean to hurt you."

Adeline sat quietly for a few seconds. "Anyways, she did," she said in a low voice. "I think it pushed me farther away from the team." She sighed. "I don't know how I'll ever feel like I'm a part of this team. I'm in a real jam.

"Mom, you're right, though," Adeline added. "I get the jitters when I'm near those two mean girls." She slapped her palm onto her open mouth and proclaimed, "And now I'll have 'em with Coach Mia!"

Her mother pulled her close and wrapped her arms around her. "You will lose that jittery feeling and you will be a part of this team, that I can promise you."

"Promise?" Adeline felt relief and hope while leaning into her mother's quiet embrace.

"If I make a promise and give you my word, it usually comes true. I don't make those unless I am sure they can happen." Mrs. Lawrence gave her daughter a gentle squeeze. She knew Adeline would hold out and find the positives at the gym. That was her way. This was a temporary stumble, and she would pick herself up and keep going.

"Right," Adeline said before taking in a slow, deep breath. Exhaling at the same unhurried pace, she felt her shoulders and chest loosening as tension flowed away, her upper body settling comfortably in her mother's strong arms.

Chapter Five

At the following gym practice Adeline gave all her attention to her routines and tried to ignore Harper and Macey.

While awaiting her turn at the bars, Adeline spoke to Olivia and Keely, the two girls who had greeted her pleasantly when she was introduced to the team.

"How long have you been at this gym?" she asked Olivia.

Olivia answered, "This is my second year here. I joined East Coast last year, after my family moved to Jacksonville from Virginia."

Brightening upon hearing these words, Adeline replied, "Then you're fairly new here."

Adeline asked Keely, "How long have *you* been here?"

"This is my third year," Keely said. "I was on the level 4 team last year, and I was on recreational before that. Macey and Harper began here the same time I did."

"Gosh, Keely," Adeline said, "I think you're much better than they are. I thought they had probably just started!"

"Well,"—Keely shrugged her shoulders dramatically, saying, with a laugh—"you can't start at level 5."

Smacking her forehead with the palm of her right hand, Adeline acknowledged her mistake. "True," she said. "I can't help being surprised, though, that they are on a level 5 team."

Keely's turn was called, and she approached the bars.

Lowering her voice, Olivia said, "Harper and Macey were brought up to level 5 because"—she leaned closer to Adeline and whispered—"Keely was moving up, and they didn't want her to advance without *them*. They started the same time *she* did, and I guess they thought they should all step up together. Actually, Keely and I were the only ones Coach Les was placing on the level 5 team."

Olivia paused to applaud Keely's excellent bar performance before she said, "Harper and Macey and their moms"—Olivia scrunched her mouth and nose, showing her disapproval—"made a big fuss about it. So here they are. Some of the other level 5 girls had to move to level 6."

Adeline's eyebrows shot up. "Wait. Doesn't the coach decide who advances?"

"Of course he does," Olivia said. "I am telling you, though, it was a *fuss*! I guess he got tired of hearing about it. Anyway," she said with a shrug, "they came up with us."

With her turn up, Adeline didn't have time to think about Olivia's words. She adjusted her hand grips and, approaching the bar, she turned back to Olivia, who gave her an encouraging wave. Harper and Macey were waiting on the far side and were staring at her.

Adeline felt her muscles quivering. She shook it off and completed a perfect glide kip onto the low bar. After the free hip, she managed a kip to squat on before jumping to the high bar with a glide kip and a cast-away long hang pullover. During the two swings, as she often did, she felt a surge of energy before she released her hands for the flyaway. Hoping to stick the landing, she faltered and took one small extra step before placing her feet together.

Tilting her head, Adeline silently questioned her coach. She knew she had performed her best on the bars, and her coach's reaction, holding two thumbs up, confirmed it.

"Olivia, you're up," Coach Les called out. "Ze rest of you, be beck een teen."

Harper and Macey followed Adeline into the snack area. They ignored her. She took her drink and moved toward Keely, who was sitting on the floor.

"Adeline," Olivia called as she entered the room. Adeline stopped abruptly and turned at the sound of her name. Olivia raised both arms high above her head as she shouted, "Adeline, awesome bar routine! Wow! I hope I can do as great one day. And soon!"

Olivia dropped her arms to grab her drink from the snack table and took the few steps to stand in front of Adeline.

"Hey, sit with us, okay?" She touched Adeline's arm and crossed a short distance to sit beside Keely.

Adeline's relief was evident when she joined them. "Thanks," she said as she lowered herself onto the floor. "You can't begin to understand how much I want to do my best here."

She directed her next words to Olivia, who had complimented her bar routine. "I mean, I'm the *new* girl, and you don't want your new teammate to be sloppy!" She laughed.

They all giggled and took sips of their water.

When Adeline raised her bottle, she caught sight of Harper and Macey watching the three of them. Adeline felt an uneasy tingling. As soon as her vision shifted to her new friends, she relaxed and the uncomfortable tingle vanished.

During the rest of the practice, Adeline stayed beside Olivia or Keely and ignored Harper and Macey. She didn't want or need their rudeness. She felt good when she was with Olivia and Keely; they were nice to her.

Adeline was getting up onto the first beam when she noticed Macey talking to Olivia at one of the other beams. Olivia was laughing at whatever Macey was saying. They were both smiling when

Harper walked up to them. When Macey saw Harper, she reacted as though she had been caught doing something wrong. She left Olivia to stand at Harper's side. Olivia took a few steps closer to them and opened her mouth, about to speak. Harper immediately put her head close to Macey's and spoke quietly to her. Harper was totally excluding Olivia!

Such rudeness, Adeline thought. *That girl has real problems.*

Adeline positioned herself on the beam and focused on the steps of her routine. After her mount, she did a back walkover, then a series of postures and poses including a lunge and quarter-turn, before moving into the rond de jambe, arabesque, and final tilt into the scale. She held it for a few seconds and chuckled. *I'm a bird!*

During the straight leg leap, Adeline knew she bent her front leg and didn't reach the appropriate height. She wobbled when her feet landed on the beam. She made a mental note: *I need to work on that.*

After the straight jump, she completed her step kick and entered the handstand. She maintained her balance for the required two seconds and returned her feet to the beam, taking a few

dramatic backward steps and moving into the half backward swing turn. She leaned to the right after making the turn, lost her balance, and jumped off the beam. *What! Again?*

Concentrate, she told herself. She quickly remounted, repeated the half backward swing turn, and moved into the split jump. She felt a wobble when she landed, made the cross step, felt a second wobble, and completed a pivot turn before entering the full turn. She leaned to her right after the turn, managed to keep upright, and stayed on the beam. A final step kick put her into the handstand and quarter-turn dismount.

"Good job, Adeline," Coach Mia called to her. "Great job, ladies," she said to all of them. She peeked at her watch. "Oops, thet's eet. See you next time."

Adeline skipped across the gym floor to the snack room to grab her things, and Olivia and Keely ran up to her side.

"We are glad you're on our team, Adeline," Olivia said.

"Yeah," Keely said. "We can sure use you."

They picked up their possessions from the table in the snack room and headed to the exit.

"Thanks," Adeline said, her upturned lips stretching from ear to ear.

"Adeline!" Olivia exclaimed. "You're absolutely beaming!"

With her wide grin dissolving into a snicker, Adeline retorted, recalling what her father said. "And you have vaulting ambition!"

Olivia shrieked with laughter, then stopped suddenly. "What does that even mean?"

"But I set the bar too low," Keely said, to continue the banter. She chortled with glee, doubling over as she laughed harder.

All were near tears—happy tears—when they strolled out the door.

Chapter Six

Adeline was feeling restless. She reclined on her comfy bed with her arms crossed under her head, staring at the ceiling. Occasionally she took in a slow, calming breath, fighting the urge to stand up. If she did get on her feet, she would only want to lie down again. She had already done that two-step jumpiness dance. And she had done it three times! She refused to do it again. *Relax*, she told herself.

She had managed to survive three months of practice in her new gym, and summer was over. In two days she'd be entering the fifth grade, and she could hardly believe it. What happened to fourth grade? Her competing in gymnastics seemed to make everything go faster, and her head was spinning with the speed of it. If she wasn't careful, it would whirl off and hit the ceiling. She cringed, imagining the sight of that!

The first qualifying meet in level 5 competition was in two weeks. Adeline had no idea how she would get through the next fourteen days.

What a summer it had been! She had become good friends with Olivia and Keely, and for that she was thankful. Harper, on the other hand, continued to shun her, ignoring her each time she tried to talk to her.

Macey was a little friendlier. Adeline and she laughed a few times over silly things that happened at the gym. When Harper was nearby, however, Macey paid all her attention to Harper.

Adeline could not understand it. *What power,* she thought. *If Harper told Macey to get on all fours and meow like a cat, Macey probably would.* Also, Adeline had noticed Olivia and Keely acting restrained when Harper was close to them.

What is it? she wondered. *How can Harper have that much power over them? Are they afraid of her?*

The first two weeks of school flew by in a hurricane of activity. Adeline liked her fifth-grade teacher and had been excited to find one of her friends from her fourth-grade class in the schoolroom.

She was telling her friend goodbye at the end of the school day on Friday when her mother pulled up.

"Last chance to clean up your routines," her mother teased when Adeline climbed into the car. "Tomorrow is showtime!"

"Mom, really?" Adeline grumbled, and fumbled for the seat belt. "Do you have to?"

"No," Mrs. Lawrence replied, "I don't have to. I simply want to." She steered the SUV away from the school and said, "How was your tenth day of fifth grade?"

Adeline welcomed the change of topic and relaxed comfortably into the seat. "Great," she said eagerly. "I love my teacher. Oh, I forgot to tell you. I have to get a story together for the school storytelling contest."

"Already? Isn't it a little early in the year?"

"Yeah, maybe ... I guess it is," Adeline answered. "My teacher told us yesterday, and I forgot to tell you last night. She wants us to begin searching for a story. First you tell it to the class, then if you win in the classroom, you tell it to the schoolkids in the auditorium." With more enthusiasm she said, "And then you go to the district level and compete against fifth graders from other schools in the district. Then if you are still in, you go to the state level, then to the national level, and then—"

"Whoa! Wait a minute, young lady," her mother said. "Isn't that going a bit too far?"

"Not if you win," Adeline said, drawing herself up taller in the seat. "And I am going to work ultrahard on this one!"

Her mother pulled up to a stop sign, and Adeline sat quietly. Her mom turned her head first to the right, then left, then right again before steering onto the highway.

After her mother sped up and was on her way, Adeline asked her, "Remember last year?"

"How could I forget?" Her mother's face showed her amusement.

Adeline had searched a long time for the perfect story. She finally gave up on finding the tale she thought would be the best and ended up telling "The Three Little Pigs." Before deciding on that story, she had presented several possibilities to her parents and little sister and became quite the storyteller!

While "The Three Little Pigs" was not a big hit with her fourth-grade classmates, Adeline's teacher had commended Adeline for her performance. Unfortunately, her story had lacked originality and creativity.

"Guess what story I'm going to tell this year?" Adeline didn't give her mom time to answer before she said, "I've selected 'The Toetally Top Toe.' "

Her mother laughed. They had read that together. It was in one of the old readers her mother had salvaged from the school's book donation pile.

In the story, the main character was admiring her beautiful feet and decided to hold a toe contest. Unfortunately, all kinds of misfortunes occurred before and during the toe-off. It was an enjoyable read.

"Yep, I will toetally do that one," Adeline said, "and I will tell it in a nice toene."

"And after you've toeld it," her mother said, "you can come home to a cheese toest snack."

They grinned at each other.

Adeline pulled out her math homework. Schoolwork was difficult to get to and she had to catch it in moments like these. She worked three problems and while multiplying two numbers on the fourth one, she heard her mother groan.

"Uh-oh," Adeline's mother said, slowing down because of a car parked on the side of the highway. A curve was not far ahead, and she had to quickly steer past the car.

As she drove by it, her mother muttered, "If a car comes around that curve, I am dead meat."

"Then what will that make me?" Adeline asked innocently. "A side dish?"

It was the big day—the first qualifying meet. Adeline, her parents, and her little sister had been in the family SUV for over an hour and were entering Gainesville, where the meet was being held.

Mrs. Lawrence's parents lived in Gainesville, and the family had made plans to spend the night with them. They were driving to their house for a short rest before going to the gym.

Adeline and Charlotte had fallen asleep, and Mr. Lawrence decided it was time to rouse them.

“Guess where we are, kids,” he said in a loud, playful tone. They had entered a familiar street, and he knew Adeline would recognize the area. He didn’t think Charlotte would. “I think Adeline will know where *she* is.”

Both girls aroused slowly, stretching a few minutes in their attempts to fully awaken themselves and, sleepy eyed, peered out the car windows. Mr. Lawrence glanced into the rearview mirror at Charlotte, who was sitting behind him. Her blond curls were flattened where her head had rested against the side of her car seat. She leaned forward to better see his reflection in the mirror, and exclaimed, “And I know where me am, Daddy!”

Mr. Lawrence showed surprise before his concentration returned to the motorway in front of him. He glimpsed her reflection in the mirror as she said, in a loud voice, “I’m right back here!”

Chapter Seven

The gym was already crowded when Adeline and her family entered. Adeline chewed on her lower lip and tightly clutched the straps of her backpack. She scanned the spacious room.

"There they are!" Adeline yelled. She quickly kissed her mother and father, who wished her good luck, and she gave her little sister the thumbs-up sign. Adeline sprinted across the gym floor.

"Hey, Coach," Adeline yelled as she approached the group.

"Vell, eet's about time," Coach Les said, spinning around. He glanced at his watch. "I vas about to get vorried."

"Sorry," she said breathlessly. "We stopped at my grandma and grandpa's house." She smiled sheepishly. "They always make such a fuss over us. I thought we'd *never* get away."

Amazed by the size of the gym, she peered up at the rafters. "Wow!" She swiveled in all directions and gazed down the rows of bleachers along the far side of the gym. "Wow! This is some gym. It reminds me of state!"

"Funny you say zet." Coach Les was unable to hide his pleasure while telling her the news. "Zees ees vhere ze state competition veell be held zees year."

"No kidding!" Adeline exclaimed. She drew in her breath. Her parents would like hearing that. Free lodging for all of them, and her grandparents would get to see her compete—*if* she made it to state. They were coming today and planned to arrive right before the team march-in.

"Ve are vasting time, girls." Coach Les became suddenly serious, clapping his hands three times. "Let's stretch."

Adeline set her backpack on the team's pile of packs and ran over to Olivia and Keely. They greeted her with elation mirroring her own.

Adeline sat with her legs folded under her, following her coach's directions.

After several minutes, she sat in a straddle position and stretched her legs as far to either side as she could. She leaned forward until her chest touched the floor and lay there, thinking about her routines. *This is it. I need to do better than ever, and I can.* She felt her nerves prickling and told herself that was okay. Being nervous gave her more energy, made her moves sharper.

Adeline sat up and stretched her legs straight out in front of her. She leaned over slowly until her chest rested on the tops of her thighs. She raised her arms and held them straight in front of her, parallel with her legs. She stretched her fingers out over her toes and felt her muscles loosening.

Coach Les gave the signal, and Adeline jumped up and ran with her teammates along the edge of the floor mat. As she jogged, she searched her competitors, who were stretching and practicing handstands and walkovers on the various dark blue floor mats.

When she sighted the level 5 team from Jacksonville Gymnastics, her heart sank. She recognized Stephanie Bard. Stephanie had been in her carpool when Adeline was on the Jacksonville Gymnastics level 4 team. Stephanie had been on the level 5 team then, and apparently still competed with that group.

Adeline recalled when Stephanie told the carpool she would get to compete in the first optional level this season and possibly move up to level 7 after that.

At the optional level, each gymnast performed their own routine and was judged according to the skills they displayed, along with their overall level and performance during the routine. They weren't judged on specific skills, like they were at other levels.

Why is Stephanie competing in level 5 again? Adeline was aghast. *I can't compete against her! It's not fair!* Then she remembered Stephanie's birthday party at the end of the season, and she realized Stephanie was in a different age group. Adeline let her breath out slowly. *That was a close one.* However, Adeline did have to compete against her own age group on the Jacksonville Gymnastics' level 5 team.

The whistle blew for the premeet run-through, and the girls gathered their gear. Coach Les led them to their first practice event, the bars.

Waiting in line behind Keely, Adeline glanced over at the stands to search for her parents and looked right into the faces of her level 4 Jacksonville Gymnastics team. They were sitting with their coach and were all staring at her.

Adeline swallowed hard, drew herself up, and waved. At the same time she could feel her nerves doing extra prickles. *Oh no,* she thought, *they'll be watching this whole competition. They are probably hoping I do horribly. After all, they wanted me to stay in level 4 with them. I'm sure they're surprised to see me on this level 5 team.*

Taking in a deep breath, she tried to stop her thoughts. Keely was finishing her bar routine drill, and Adeline was next. She felt a flush creeping up her neck; she could feel all the level 4 girls' eyes on her.

Coach Les waved her on, and she jumped up to the low bar and executed a perfect glide kip. *Nothing new, I had that last year.* Adeline skipped to the next glide kip to squat on and quickly jumped forward to the high bar. She practiced the two swings and felt the increase in energy, enabling her to complete the flyaway with no problem. Maybe too much energy. She had trouble sticking the landing and fell forward, catching herself on the mat with outstretched arms. *Nooooo, not now!*

She jumped up and, although she felt embarrassed, she faked a grin for her coach, who always expected a good attitude.

"I'm not vorried," Coach Les told her. "You'll lend eet vhen you need to." He added, "I've never eveen seen you fall before."

The rest of the practice events went without mishap. Adeline felt she had done well enough, despite some obvious mistakes. *Something to work on during the meet,* she thought. She had forgotten who was there watching her and she was enjoying the spirit of the big competition.

Finally, it was time for the march-in. Adeline and her teammates joined the others assembling outside the competing area. There they found the excitement in the air staggering. And there they witnessed a communal alertness and energy that tied them all together.

The teams moved forward for the march-in, and Adeline's insides were vibrating. She glanced at Olivia and Keely, who seemed to share the exhilaration she felt. Harper and Macey were in front of them. As their team neared the main gym, they formed a single line and followed three other teams.

When they entered the large gym, a young girl stepped in front of them and led them to a designated spot. Adeline's team waited in a straight line, while the other teams filed in and took their places. Soon, all the teams were lined up across the floor in columns. Adeline stood behind Olivia, and they both bounced on the balls of their feet.

The music stopped, and the announcer called out the name of a team, followed by the individual team members' names. Adeline heard the announcement of East Coast Gymnastics and waited for her name. When she heard it, she raised her arms high in salute and grinned in the direction of what sounded to her like heavy applause. She lowered her arms and fixed her gaze on the source of the cheers.

Her family, including her grandparents, were seated in the bleachers. Next to her mom was Harper's mother. Adeline recognized her instantly. She had seen her with Harper many times at the gym.

Adeline looked down the rows of people to the area where the level 4 team had congregated. They were still there.

I may not score all that great today—not with these jitters. Anyways, though, at least I've proven I can do this level. 'Cause here I am!

Chapter Eight

The whistle blew for the meet to begin, and Adeline and her teammates stretched taller with heads raised as they walked proudly to their first event, the bars. After greeting the judges, Adeline frowned at the bars. She liked to do the bars event either halfway through the competition or at the end. She usually felt the most energetic after the second or third event, and she needed that energy to get through the bar routine.

Coach Les pulled Adeline aside and told her to put on her hand grips, and then he called out the lineup. Adeline was fourth. That meant she'd be first on the next event, the beam. *Not good!* She groaned. *I am in trouble!*

While a girl from a different gym took her place at the lower bar, Adeline pulled at her grips. *Where is my energy?* She bounced slightly and tried to muster up some *oomph.*

"Okay, Adeline," Coach Les finally called when it was her turn.

Standing in front of the low bar, she waited for the signal from the judges. One waved at her, and Adeline saluted with arms stretched high toward the ceiling. She positioned herself, lunged, grabbed the low bar, and did a perfect glide kip before completing her cast. She felt herself weakening, yet managed the free hip with minimal struggle. *Points off,* she thought.

After the next kip, she squatted onto the low bar and jumped to the high bar into a kip, to a cast, and into the long hang pullover. *Thank you, baby giant!* she said to herself, knowing it wasn't a true one. She then took a swing forward, then backward, then forward into the flyaway.

This time Adeline maintained her footing and turned with a big grin and saluted the judges. She could hear the applause and her family's cheers, and she flashed a wider smile. It wasn't a great routine. However, she knew it would bring her a decent score.

She sat and waited. Finally, the number flashed on a small screen set up near the bars. She scored 8.15. *Not bad, for my first level 5 bar routine.* She knew her scores would improve at each meet, and she was satisfied to start with a score of 8 or better.

After taking off her grips, Adeline noticed the beginning of a rip on one of her callouses. To avoid thinking about it, she gave her full attention to the girls on the uneven bars. After the last East Coast girl finished, Adeline realized with surprise that her score was the highest on the team.

Olivia, Keely, and Macey scored high 7s, with Harper scoring 6.65. Harper had dropped from the high bar before she could complete the second swing. She had been having trouble with her grips, and she left the bars, complaining her grips hurt her.

"Next rotation," the announcer said loudly. "Vault to bars, bars to beam, beam to floor, floor to vault."

The team moved as one, all picking up their backpacks and bottles and dropping them on a pile at the beam. Adeline stood with her teammates in front of the judges. She smiled and said "Hi," along with the others. She took her place.

"Okay, Adeline." Coach Les stepped over to her. "Just do eet ze same vay you hev done eet et our gym. You hev excellent beam routine and you need to show eet to zees crowd."

She raised her head and said, "I'll try, Coach."

The judges waved at Adeline, and she saluted them. She approached the wooden beam and pressed her hands on top of the smooth suede padding. She swung herself up into the initial mount and completed the first positions without any trouble. She held her body straight and tall, completing the next movements with no more than slight faltering.

After another moment of positions and turns, Adeline felt as though she was one with the beam. All else was forgotten. When it was time to do the handstand, she raised her legs with ease and held them perfectly. She held them a little longer, and even longer.

Okay, Adeline thought. *Come down, legs … anytime now.* She was frozen! Her legs were suspended in time and they held fast where they were. *Anytime now!* she ordered. Despite her command, her legs kept their fixed position.

She was beginning to worry her legs would never come down. Finally, after a few more seconds—feeling like ten minutes—Adeline's legs toppled over and, to keep from falling, she jumped to the floor.

No-no-no, she groaned to herself, but she had to finish the routine. She hopped onto the beam and with shaking legs she repeated the handstand. Because she was afraid it would happen a second time, she raised her feet up for a quick touch and immediately brought them down.

As she tried to overcome the churning in her stomach, she moved through the half backward swing turn with some wobbling—no leaning—and completed a perfect split jump. She stumbled on the full turn, made it to the step kick, and stuck the handstand dismount.

You goof, she scolded herself after she saluted the judges. *You fall over on a simple handstand, yet you stick the split jump!*

Adeline trudged to where Coach Les was standing, and he smiled at her with encouragement, showing his support.

"Zet hendstend deedn't vant to let go," he said, placing his hand on her shoulder. "Vhat a beautiful spleet jump, zough. Don't vorry. You veell hev eet all next time."

Coach Les stayed beside Adeline as they waited for the results. They were silent when the screen flashed her identifying number and score.

Oops, she thought, *never have I ever had points this low.* A bright 7.0 shone on the board for all the world to see, and she groaned inwardly. *I will have to do impossibly great on the floor and vault to end up with any kind of a decent overall score.*

Her coach squeezed her shoulder before he dropped his hand. "Next time," he reminded her.

Adeline got through her next two events without another thought of her beam routine and scored 8.8 on the floor event and 8.0 on the vault. She realized with surprise that she had barely missed the overall score she needed to be eligible for the state competition. She missed it by 5/100 of a point. She didn't know whether to be happy or sad. She was surprised she had gotten that close, which made her happy. Missing the needed score by 5/100 of a point, though, made her sad.

After the closing ceremony, Adeline met up with her parents and grandparents. Harper's mother was with them.

"Adeline," her mother said when they were close to her. "This is Harper's mother, Mrs. Johnson." Adeline's mom gave her daughter the "It's fine" face.

"Congratulations," Harper's mother said before Adeline could reply.

Adeline was puzzled. "Excuse me," she said, "did you say congratulations?"

"Yes, I did," Mrs. Johnson replied. "You made a qualifying score to move up to level 6. We don't really care that much at our gym about qualifying for state. That's merely another meet. It's more important for the girls to show they have the skills and can move on up to develop more skills. You did great, Adeline."

With that good news, Adeline's happy-sad conflict was over! "Thank you," she said. *Wow, I'm going on to level 6, for sure!* Peering behind Mrs. Johnson, Adeline caught sight of Olivia and Keely racing toward her with ear-to-ear smiles.

They were shouting, "Adeline, you are our top scorer! You are the only one that scored over 31 today. You get to go on to level 6 after the season!"

Adeline grinned. "That's what Mrs. Johnson was telling me." Adeline giggled. "I guess that makes up for the grand handstand on the beam!"

Olivia and Keely erupted into laughter.

Chapter Nine

On the way to her grandparents' house, Adeline asked her mother if they could have sweet tea with dinner.

"Oh no!" her mother exclaimed. "Not again!"

"Yeah, I noticed one after my bar routine," Adeline replied.

"What are you two talking about?" her father interjected.

"Adeline places hot tea bags on her rips when she gets them," Mrs. Lawrence told her husband. "It helps protect and harden the open blisters." And to Adeline she said, "Of course, we'll make sure you have a hot tea bag treatment tonight, with the bonus of sweet tea with dinner."

"The bonus helps me do it," Adeline told her dad. "The tea bags really sting at first!"

Adeline changed the subject, and her enthusiasm overflowed while she talked about her performance.

"I can't believe I came in third on the floor event, with an 8.8." She held up her ribbon. "Mom and Dad, I'm so excited!" Her voice lowered when she said, "Though I hated it when I fell off the beam." She shook her head. "I still can't believe my overall score."

She cried, "My gosh, think what my overall score would have been if I hadn't fallen off the beam! Mom, I might have scored 33, or,"—she touched her fingers to her open mouth—"close to 34, and maybe I—"

"Whoa." Her father stopped her in mid-sentence. "Slow down, Adeline. You're getting ahead of yourself. You did what you did today, and during the next event you'll do what you do then. There's no 'what if I had,' because you didn't, and next time you may or may not."

"What?" Adeline said. "You lost me, Dad."

"I am simply saying there is no point in thinking about 'what if I had done such and such,' because if you say 'what if,' then it must not have happened, and if it didn't happen, then there is no point in considering it, and—"

"Okay, okay, Dad, I get your point," Adeline said. "Why do you always have to be so tech …." She struggled for the word and gave it another try. "Techo ... I mean … technological?"

"Uh … Adeline." Her father peered into the rearview mirror at her. "Don't you mean technical?"

"Whatever." Adeline grinned at his reflection.

Directing a question to her mother's head, Adeline said, "Mom, did you realize that was Harper's mother when she sat next to you?"

"Yes, I did. You pointed Harper out to me several weeks ago, and I saw her mother. Anyhow, I had assumed it was her picking up Harper at the gym."

Mrs. Lawrence twisted in her seat, giving her full attention to her daughter, and added, "Harper's mother had lots to say."

"Unlike her daughter," Adeline grumbled.

Her mom laughed and said, "No, I mean she had lots to say about Harper."

Mrs. Lawrence's voice took on a serious tone. "She's worried about her. She was telling me that Harper's father asked for a divorce six months ago, and Harper has not been the same since he left their home."

Adeline's mom waited for a reaction. When Adeline showed little change in her facial expression, Mrs. Lawrence said, "Mrs. Johnson is having trouble with her. She said Harper becomes angry easily and she's hard to handle. Mrs. Johnson knows her daughter is unhappy, but I think they are both suffering and—"

"Okay, Mom. I get the picture," Adeline said, breaking her off.

"This is serious, Adeline," her mother replied. "I think Harper is depressed, and I think her mother is, also. Their home life has been disrupted. I am sure they are each having difficulty coping with this change in the family."

Adeline did not respond. She sat quietly, with her head down, studying her hands.

"Don't you get it, Adeline?" Mrs. Lawrence said with a raised voice.

Adeline looked up. Their eyes met.

"Harper is a very unhappy little girl."

Wincing at the "little girl" part, Adeline stared blankly at her mother.

"And she's struggling with what life has brought her," her mom said. "She is angry at her parents, angry at herself, and she takes it out on less threatening individuals. Like you."

Adeline averted her eyes and gazed out the window. She wondered what it would be like if her father left without a warning or, for that matter, left *with* a warning. Tears bubbled up. She loved her father, and she knew she would not be able to bear such a thing. *Poor Harper. How awful that must be for her. No wonder she's acting like she is.*

And the way she behaves towards me has nothing to do with me. I thought she didn't like me, but this is about her. Not me.

At her second meet, Adeline felt no pressure and managed to stay on the beam. She was excited about her overall score of 33.35 and couldn't wait until the state meet. However, she had a third meet to go through first.

Harper continued to be a problem. Adeline felt the jitters each time she entered the same room.

Nevertheless, Adeline decided to be nice to her. Harper's rudeness showed itself every time Adeline was friendly, and Adeline was ready to ditch the whole "being nice" thing. Biting her tongue when Harper made mean remarks, Adeline made herself think about Harper's home situation.

More and more, Adeline was seeing the anger she suspected was within Harper. That only made Adeline feel worse for her. Harper seemed mixed-up and confused, and after Adeline knew the reason for the bad-mannered behavior, she was unable to get upset with her teammate.

During the last practice before the third meet, Keely was talking with Adeline about her scores.

"Adeline, you got the best score at the first meet *and* the second one. I'm going to beat you next time," Keely teased.

"You go right ahead," Adeline replied. "I'd like to have you with me at state."

Keely attained the score to move up to level 6, but she had not yet accomplished the number needed to qualify for the state competition.

"That will never happen," a voice sneered from behind.

They spun around. Harper was glaring at them.

"She can't make over a 31." With a wicked grin, she added, "Keely barely has her kip."

Adeline could handle Harper's insult when it was directed at her, but she didn't like seeing her go off on any of the other girls. They didn't understand Harper, and they were clearly more disturbed by what she said.

Keely's shoulders drooped and she lowered her head. She shifted from one foot to the other and stared at the floor.

Adeline started to bristle. She shook it off and went to Keely's side, placing an arm across her friend's shoulders. Adeline ignored Harper and led Keely away from her.

"That's not true, Keely," she whispered. "Don't let Harper get to you. She's having troubles, and I think she needs our help. We're gonna have to ignore her meanness. While that might be impossible,"—Adeline stated her last word slowly, and then raised her vocal pitch—"we have to at least try."

Keely chuckled before her voice dropped. "She is right, you know. I barely do have my kip. Sometimes it's there and at other times," she added, in a mysterious tone, "I think somebody's stolen it!"

"I can tell you one thing." Adeline snickered. "Harper is certainly not the thief! Have you seen *her* kip lately?"

Keely giggled with Adeline as they strode to the next practice area.

When Harper joined the group a few minutes later, she glanced at Adeline. Adeline gave her a direct look and a weak smile. Harper blushed before she looked away.

Chapter Ten

Adeline's performance at the third meet improved her overall score to 34.00, and she was pleased with the progress she'd made. She was more delighted that Olivia and Keely achieved the scores needed for both level 6 and the state competition. Harper and Macey were also moving up to level 6 and would be competing at state.

"We did it!" Keely slapped Adeline's outstretched hands with a double high five at the end of the meet. They kept their arms up and began dancing, moving rhythmically toward the gym's exit, singing, "We did it. We did it. We really, really did it!"

"Of course, what did you expect? Did you ever doubt it?" Adeline hugged her friend. "I knew you wouldn't send me to state all alone."

"*I* certainly doubted it!" Harper said behind them, and Adeline and Keely twirled at once. Harper frowned at Keely. "I really don't think you are ready for state."

Adeline's chin jutted out as she clenched her fists. "She's as ready as you are!" She glared at Harper, her nostrils flaring. "Harper, how can you continue to be so mean and hateful to all of us? What have we ever done to you? You have never said one nice word to me since I came here, and I'll bet you've never said one nice thing to anyone in your *life*!" Adeline was yelling. Feeling the rise of her emotions, she mentally questioned her reaction. *Where is this coming from? Is this the red-headed temper Mom didn't think I had?*

"I have had it!" Adeline shouted in exasperation before curbing her voice an octave lower. "You know, I even liked you for a while, but you sure make it hard—" Adeline stopped in the middle of her sentence, seeing lines of tears splashing down Harper's cheeks. *Finally,* she thought, *this girl has feelings!* Adeline stood in front of Harper, breathing heavily, not knowing what to say.

Harper sat down, making muffled, crying sounds, and Adeline felt guilty she had caused her to cry. Harper wrapped her arms around her drawn-up knees and laid her head on them. Her shoulders shook rhythmically with her sobbing.

Other gymnasts were staring as they passed. Harper didn't seem to notice.

Adeline's eyes grew larger and she gawked at Keely, seeing Keely's same wide-eyed look.

What if Harper goes hysterical on us?

Crouching down, Adeline touched Harper's arm. "Harper," she said gently, "I didn't mean to upset you. I just wanted you to understand—"

"Understand what?" Harper snapped her head up, her tone sharp.

Lowering her head again, she muttered, "It's *you* who doesn't understand. I get it. I'm hateful, always saying the wrong things to you all. I realize how awful I am, but I don't know why I say those things. I'm just *ultra mad* at everybody! I'm mad at *all* of you *all* the time!"

Adeline gingerly squeezed Harper's arm. She disliked seeing anyone cry. "Harper, I'm sure there's a reason for that. Maybe something else is making you mad, and maybe we're the only ones you can let it out on."

Harper raised her head slightly, her watery eyes meeting Adeline's, her surprise showing in them. Their eyes locked a few seconds, and then Harper switched her gaze and peered into the distant corner of the room. She stared off for a moment, appearing to be in deep thought.

Adeline waited. Keely quietly sat down across from them.

After another moment or two, Harper turned to Adeline. "I *have* been letting it out on you, haven't I?" She smiled sheepishly. "Gosh, I've been such a jerk! I've needed friends more than ever, and I've done nothing but push you all away."

She placed her fingertips over her closed eyelids and sighed heavily. "And you've always been so nice to me," she said quietly, peeking out at Adeline. "And you, same," directing her words at Keely.

Harper sat quietly for a minute, then brought her hands forward. She saw the tear streaks on her fingertips. She laughed, exclaiming, "*I* must *look* lovely!"

Keely and Adeline grinned at her, and as Adeline realized she had never seen Harper smile, much less laugh, she remarked, "Harper, you've never looked better!"

"Thanks a lot!" Harper leaned and jabbed Adeline's side with her elbow.

"Think nothing of it!" Adeline lowered from a crouch to a sitting position in one quick movement and as she did, she bumped into Harper's side with exaggerated vigor.

"I think you're gorgeous!" Keely yelled while placing her hands on the floor behind her and gently pushing her foot against Harper's chest.

Harper toppled rearward, catching herself before she fell, screaming, "And thank *you*!"

"Sure thing!" Keely gave a second push and missed.

Adeline shrieked, "I think you're as pretty as an arabesque!" She fell over sideways and rolled onto her back, kicking her legs in the air.

They fell helplessly into laughter.

Adeline lay with the others, laughing the loudest and smiling broadly as she realized that life with Harper just had a restart and a friendship was blossoming. It wouldn't matter how they scored at

state. That was merely a final performance of their level 5 routine. They were going on to level 6!

What a season it had been! Adeline sat in the rear seat of her mother's SUV as the family pulled away from the state competition in Gainesville. She felt tired after all the hype leading up to state and the excitement during the competition.

Keely recovered the stolen kip. The thief was her lack of confidence. After it had taken the kip, Keely outsmarted the burglar. She had to believe it was still in her and told herself that every day. When she struggled with it in a practice, she exclaimed aloud, "Oh no you don't, lack of confidence! It's mine and you won't steal it! Never again!"

When that happened, she'd get up on the bars and repeat the routine, and presto! The kip was there for her. Slowly, her confidence grew, and she nailed it every time.

Adeline smiled to herself. She recalled Keely's excitement when she placed number one in the uneven bars event an hour earlier. Keely was thrilled when she accepted the state first place medal, and it was obvious her hard work and the belief that she could do it had paid off. Adeline was proud of her friend.

Resting her head on the seat back, Adeline let her eyelids drop, thinking of Harper. After the third meet and their breakdown into hilarity, Harper seemed to try at being nicer during the next practices. She was still moody at times, and Adeline had wished she could do something for her.

Mrs. Lawrence agreed to have Harper, Keely, Macey, and Olivia spend the night at their house. Late that evening Harper broke down and told the other four girls about her parents splitting up.

As she let her tears loose, she exclaimed, "I've never cried about it like *this*!"

The girls made a circle with Harper in the center, all reaching out to touch and console her. Harper cried until she couldn't.

After she blew her nose and washed her face, Harper hugged each of them and said, "I am so glad you are my friends."

At the next practice, Harper was more relaxed. She greeted Adeline and pulled her to the beam to work with her.

Wow, Adeline thought, *I never saw that coming!*

When Adeline giggled suddenly, her mother glanced backward. She remained silent when she caught a glimpse of her daughter deep in thought, eyes closed.

Adeline was picturing Harper's delight when she received the state first place medal for her floor routine. Harper had worked harder at the last few practices and she *was* good on the floor. Adeline was happy Harper made the highest score.

Somehow, with all that was going on within the team, Adeline had not pressured herself about *her* performance. In addition to working hard, she felt she had given a part of herself to the other girls. Their confidence grew along with their skills.

As did hers. Not in leaps and bounds, and she now realized why. She had focused on the team and skill building within that group, not solely on her own improvement. It gave her a good feeling. They were finally a real team! *Hurray!* She giggled, keeping herself from shouting it out aloud. She let her inner voice take over: *Hurray!*

Winning the state level 5 first place medal in beam—no leaning, no handstand freeze—should have been enough for Adeline. Likewise, being on a level 6 team should have been enough. Yet what she wanted, as much as all that, was a team working together and being there for each other. Being nice to each other. Supporting each other. Caring about each other.

She had found that team.

Keep up with Adeline on her webpage at

MarthaLouise.net/Adeline

DISCUSSION GUIDE

This discussion guide is provided for parents, teachers, and counselors to stimulate discussions on feelings and emotions and talk further about conflict resolution. The first section includes discussion questions; the next section uses sentence stems for eliciting responses. Your child may prefer one format over the other, so both are supplied. You can read or have your child read each item and allow time for their response and additional discussion.

1. Adeline had fears related to moving to a new gym. What was she afraid of? What helped her overcome those fears? Have you ever moved to a new place? What were you afraid of? What did you do to feel better?

2. How did Adeline feel when the two girls ignored her? Do you ever feel that way? What do you do when that happens?

3. Adeline felt nervous at times. What made her feel that way? Do you ever have jitters? What does that feel like? What has helped you in those situations?

4. Do you think Adeline was brave when she confronted Harper? When you feel afraid, what do you try to do? What helps you feel brave? Was Harper a bully? Why or why not?

5. Harper displayed what is known as *displaced anger*. She is angry because her parents are getting divorced. Her anger doesn't have anything to do with her friends. Yet, she treated them poorly. Discuss.

6. Keeley lost her confidence with her kip, but she did not give up. How did she get it back? If you lost your confidence, what would you do?

7. Harper's attitude caused Adeline to think Harper did not like her. Have you ever felt this way? Or if others have picked on you, did you think something was wrong with you? When Adeline heard about Harper's home troubles, she realized Harper's behavior had nothing to do with her and that Harper was reacting to her home situation. Discuss.

8. People from various countries speak different languages and when English is their second language, they may speak words with an accent. Do you know anyone who has an accent? Did you have trouble understanding Coach Les, like Adeline did? She had to focus and concentrate on his words when he spoke. Maybe you had to concentrate when you read his statements. How do you think another person feels when they look, sound, or act different? What would you do to include them and help them feel accepted? How would you encourage others to treat them fairly and respectfully?

Sentence Completion

1. Change can be challenging, but it can also be exciting. If I moved to a new place, I would be afraid that ______________________________. Even though I might be scared, I would try to ______________________________________.

2. If two girls ignored me the way they did Adeline, I would feel ______________________________. When that happens, I ______________________.

3. When I am nervous, I feel ______________.Each time I have the jitters, it helps me shake them off when I ______________________________.

4. I feel afraid when ________________________. When I feel scared, I try to _______________. What helps me feel brave is _______________.

5. An example of displaced anger is when someone can't direct their anger toward the person who

has stirred up those feelings and takes their anger out on a person or thing that poses less risk. I have shown this type of anger when I was mad at ______________________________, but took it out on ______________________________________.

6. If I lost my confidence, I would try to __________ ____.

7. When someone is mean to me, I feel __________ ___________. I know their behavior has nothing to do with me and belongs to them. Something else may be causing their unhappiness. The next time someone picks on me, I will ______________ ____.

8. People who look, sound, or act different may feel ____. To help them feel accepted and included, I can ____. I will encourage others to treat them fairly and respectfully by _____________________________.

GYMNASTICS TERMS

While these are not intended to be highly technical definitions, this glossary will give readers an idea of each term's meaning. The author thanks Tish Negron, coach, Atlanta North Stars Gymnastics, for her review.

all-around: A category that includes all the events. The gymnast earning the highest total score in all combined events wins the all-around.

arabesque: The gymnast's body is bent forward from the hip while the gymnast is standing on one leg and extending the other leg behind about 45 degrees, with arms outstretched at the sides. From this pose, the gymnast can move into the scale (see *scale*).

back hip circle: Usually performed in combination with a cast on the uneven bars. The gymnast rests on the bar in a front support, casts away, returns to the bar and travels around it, returning to a front support position.

back walkover: The gymnast starts in a standing position, leans back and makes a bridge, arching with both hands on the floor or beam and one leg going up and over in motion at the same time. The other leg follows and ends in the lunge position with both feet on the floor or beam.

cast: The gymnast begins in a front support position with hips at the bar and pushes hips off the bar, driving the legs behind the gymnast, up and away from the bar, above horizontal.

cross step: Take a step with one foot crossing over the other, to move forward, backward, or sideways.

flyaway dismount (including a tuck): On the high bar, at the bottom of the tap swing, the gymnast starts to bring knees into a tuck, releases hands from bar as their body moves upward into a backward somersault in the tuck position, landing on two feet.

free hip: Also known as a **clear hip circle** and **back hip circle**. The gymnast pulls up onto the bar, swings their body under it, then brings the body back up and over the bar for a complete rotation. The hips do not touch the bar.

front support: The gymnast rests the body on the bar, with hands shoulder-width apart, fingers pointing forward, hands wrapped around the bar, and presses up to straight arms, keeping body tense and straight.

full turn: A 360-degree turn while standing in relevé on one foot. **Standing in relevé** means standing on the ball of the foot, with the body making a straight line from the knee to the ball of the foot.

glide: (see *kip.*)

grips: A strip of leather material that covers the palms of the hands and is attached to a Velcro strip that wraps around the wrist and has holes for the fingers. Grips are worn on the hands for gymnastics activities on the uneven bars, to protect hands from rips.

half backward swing turn: The gymnast raises one leg while on the beam, swings it down and back up as the gymnast turns the other foot (pivots) and faces the opposite direction.

half-turn: Turning the full body and facing the opposite direction.

handstand: The gymnast's arms are down, head down, arms extended with hands on beam, arms supporting weight, legs pointing to the ceiling. Level 5 gymnasts hold the first handstand on the beam for two seconds.

handstand and quarter-turn dismount: The gymnast moves into a handstand, then makes a quick turn to the side while popping legs down, landing on their feet with the side of their body to the beam.

jump to high bar: The gymnast jumps from the low bar and grabs the high bar with both hands.

kip: The gymnast grabs the bar with two hands, swings forward below the bar, extending legs in pike or straddle position (glide), lifts toes back on the bar (pike-up), then pulls the bar up to their body (pull up your pants) as they swing backward to finish on top of the bar in a front support position.

long hang kip: The gymnast has hands on the high bar, swings forward with body hanging below the bar, then back and up to a front support on the bar.

long hang pullover: The gymnast swings forward with body hanging below the bar, pulling body forward, under the bar and up, flipping backward over the bar with hips square and legs straight, to rest torso on top of the bar, shift the hands to cast, to front support. It differs from baby giant pullover, in which the hands must shift before the torso makes contact with the bar.

lunge: The gymnast's front leg is bent at the knee and the back leg is straight. It is a position that most acrobatic skills, such as handstand, cartwheel, front or back walkover, and more, land in.

mount: The act of getting onto the balance beam and uneven bars and the skill used to do it.

optionals: Levels 6 through 10 are also optional levels, meaning all gymnasts choosing this option have different routines and are not judged on the specifics of the routine. Instead, they are scored based on the skills displayed and their overall level and performance.

pike: The gymnast's body is bent forward at the waist, with the legs extended straight; the gymnast's knees are close to the chest, but the legs bend at the hips only and the knees remain straight.

pivot turn: Also known simply as **pivot**. The gymnast turns the body without traveling, on one foot or both feet, swiveling in place during the pivot turn.

posture: Typically refers to position and/or body form before, during, and after executing a given skill or dance element.

pullover: The gymnast holds on to the bar, raises the body with the chin over the bar (chin up position) while keeping the body straight, then raises the legs into pike position and pulls the legs and hips up and over the bar, with the upper body rotating under the bar, ending with straight arms and straight body, upper thighs touching the bar.

quarter-turn: A turn of the body to one side; a ¼ turn, or 90 degrees.

recreational: Gymnastics as a recreational activity; for those not wishing to compete in the sport or for those getting ready for competitive gymnastics.

rond de jambe: A circular movement of the leg.

scale: To make the arabesque into a scale, the gymnast keeps lifting the back leg until it is horizontal with the shoulders and hips.

split jump: A jump straight up with one leg extended forward and one extended backward.

squat on: The gymnast brings both feet up to the low bar in squat position, in preparation for a jump to the high bar.

step kick: Just like it sounds, take a step with one leg, then kick with the other.

stick: To land an acrobatic skill, jump, or dismount perfectly, without any steps, stumbles, or errors.

straddle: The gymnast's legs are spread apart, typically with legs facing upward and torso upright.

straight jump: A jump straight up with both feet, landing in the same spot.

straight leg leap: The body moves straight up and forward with both legs, taking off with one leg and landing on the opposite leg, typically requiring 180 degrees of leg separation.

tap swing: The gymnast swings, holding on to the high bar, in a hollow position, but shows a slight arch at the bottom of the swing (the feet stop while the hips and upper body continue to swing, making an arch). The body goes back quickly to the straight-hollow body position on the upswing.

tilt into scale: The gymnast lowers the upper body while in the arabesque.

tuck: The gymnast bends the knees and hips and draws the knees into the chest, as close to the body as possible.

uneven bars: One low and one high bar, with the lower bar also used for jumping to the higher bar.

About Adeline

Adeline is an acronym for:

A uthentic
D aring
E ncouraging
L oyal
I nclusive
N atural
E mpathetic

To learn more about Adeline, visit:

MarthaLouise.net/Adeline

About the Author

A retired school psychologist, Martha Louise writes children's stories to encourage prosocial behavior, hoping to instill kindness, empathy, and compassion in our young. Martha lives on one of Florida's barrier islands between the Intracoastal Waterway and the Atlantic Ocean. She has three grown daughters—two have scattered to Chicago and Ireland, and one recently moved back to Florida. When her children were younger, they were active in sports and the arts, and Martha includes their challenges in her true-to-life fictional stories. The author hopes her writing will help children gain strength and confidence in case they encounter similar circumstances. Visit her website:

MarthaLouise.net

About the Illustrator

Carol Watson lives in Russellville, Arkansas, and has been creating oil paintings for sixteen years. She painted the cover illustration for her sister's memoir. When Martha asked Carol to illustrate a children's book, the artist had reservations and a bad case of the jitters. She felt her drawing ability was lacking. However, after she recalled the enjoyment of looking at pictures in books while reading with her children and grandchildren, she decided to do it. She wants to bring that same joy to others in this story, which she hopes will inspire more kindness and understanding in our world.

A note to parents, teachers, and counselors:

Adeline in a Gymnastics Jam is not just a fictional book. Embedded in the story are practical coping skills applied to conflicts based on real-life situations. The author's goal of instilling empathy and compassion, as well as fostering social-emotional intelligence, parallels the current trend that focuses on diversity and inclusion and the acceptance of all people. Children can be kind and caring. They can learn at an early age that we are all unique and that differences are to be embraced, not ridiculed. They can also treat others with respect and help them feel they are part of the community, whether it be in a classroom, neighborhood, or in a sport or other team environment.

Included in this book is a discussion guide for parents to use with their young reader or for the older reader to go through unassisted. The guide's purpose is to stimulate discussion on feelings and emotions while encouraging prosocial behavior. Perspective-taking and empathy—important elements in the development of prosocial behavior—are reinforced throughout the guide since they generate the ability to act toward others in a positive, accepting, and supportive manner.

For those who do not participate in gymnastics, a glossary of gymnastics terms is included. Though not highly technical, the glossary will give these readers a better understanding of the postures and positions.

Lastly, the author intentionally used advanced vocabulary words to challenge the reader and stimulate vocabulary growth. The addition of clues and outright meanings within the context helps in alleviating frustration for the younger reader while encouraging and enriching vocabulary development for all readers.

Please join me in a united goal to encourage and instill kindness, compassion, inclusiveness, and empathy in our young. Together we can make our world a better community for all.

Made in the USA
Middletown, DE
28 January 2025

70478485R00062